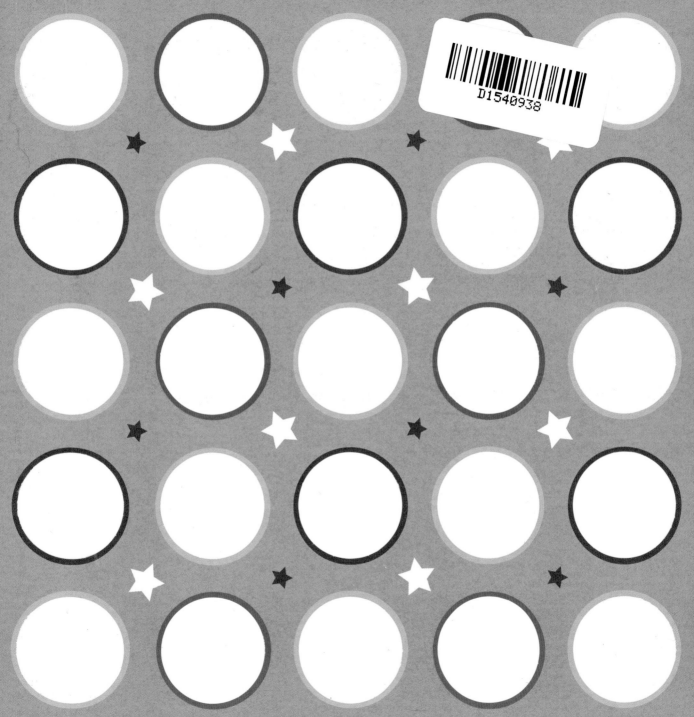

Customer Service: 1-877-277-9441 or customerservice@pikidsmedia.com

Published by Phoenix International Publications, Inc.
8501 West Higgins Road   59 Gloucester Place
Chicago, Illinois 60631   London W1U 8JJ

PI Kids and *we make books come alive* are trademarks of
Phoenix International Publications, Inc., and are registered in the United States.

www.pikidsmedia.com

ISBN: 978-1-5037-5487-4

The Twins Take Turns

A STORY ABOUT FAIRNESS

we make books come alive®
Phoenix International Publications, Inc.
Chicago • London • New York • Hamburg • Mexico City • Sydney

"Good morning, Millie and Melody,"

Minnie calls cheerfully. "Time for breakfast."

Minnie's nieces hurry to the table for their favorite meal of the day.

"I'll have some Toasted Crispy Coconut Curlies, please," says Melody.

"Me too!" says Millie.

"Oh, dear," says Minnie.
"There's only enough cereal for one.
Or you two could
share what's left."

"No," says Millie. "I'll have the cereal this morning because Melody had it yesterday."

"No fair!" says Melody. She holds on tightly to the box and…

OOps!

After breakfast, the girls get ready for school.

"I'm taking the yellow backpack today," says Melody.

Millie grabs the strap.

"It's my turn to take it," says Melody.

TUG!

"But it goes better with **my dress.**"

TUG!

"Hurry!" calls Minnie.
"The school bus is here!"
"Oh, just take it," says
Millie. "I don't want to be late."

At school, Melody chooses to do the

Colorful Carnations

science experiment.

"I can't wait to see the white flowers change **colors**!" she says.

"That's what I was going to do," says Millie.

"But I remembered to bring the **food coloring**," says Melody. "It's right here in my backpack."

"You mean **MY** backpack!" says Millie.

Miss Clarabelle comes by. **"There's no need to argue,"**
she says. "We have **so many** science experiments to choose from."

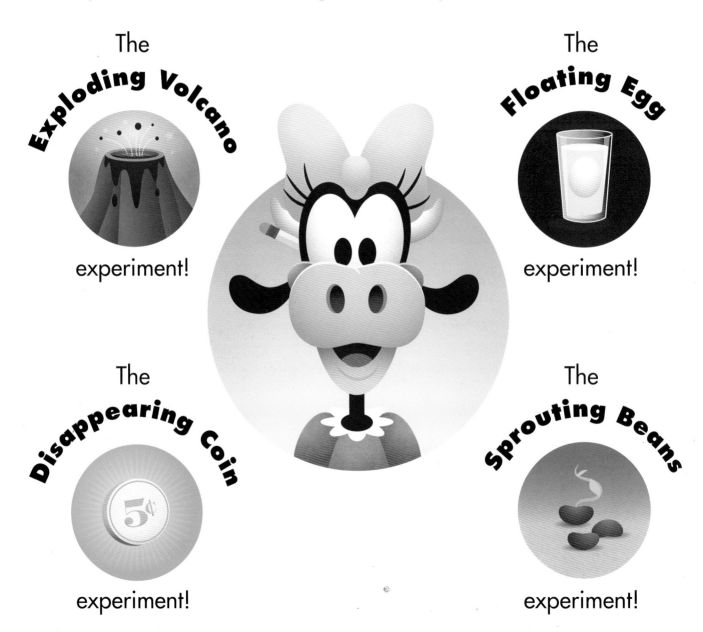

The **Exploding Volcano** experiment!

The **Floating Egg** experiment!

The **Disappearing Coin** experiment!

The **Sprouting Beans** experiment!

"Ooh, I'll choose the beans," says Millie. "I always wanted to grow a beanstalk!"
"Me too," says Melody.

After science class, the girls
go to the school library. Minnie and
Goofy are leading **story time**.

"What should we read?"
Goofy asks.

Plonk!

"**Whoops!**"

Melody raises her hand. But before Goofy can call on her, Millie jumps up and shouts,

"Little Red Riding Hood!"

Melody frowns. "That's what I was going to say."

"Good," says Minnie. "You both like the same story."

"But it was my idea first!" says Melody.

"Can someone lend a hand?" asks Goofy.

At recess, the girls join their classmates for a **jump-rope** contest. Melody cuts in line to go first. Before the other girls can ask her to stop, she takes a turn.

JUMP!
JUMP!
JUMP!

"Melody," says Millie,
"you don't **play fair**."
"Well," Melody says,
"neither do you!"

Later, at the school festival, the girls compete for

a special prize.

SPIN THE WHEEL
**WIN A
PRIZE**

"I win!"

says Millie. "I choose the teddy bear."

"I win too!"

says Melody. "And I want the teddy bear."

"Oh, no," says Millie. "You should take a water bottle since you don't have one."

"No fair!" says Melody.

After the festival, everyone
goes to the park.
Millie ignores the rules and
cuts in line for the slide.

"No fair!" says Huey.

Melody ignores the rules and cuts in line for the climbing wall.

"No fair!" says Louie.

Then, Millie and Melody **both** cut in line for the swings.

"**No fair!**" says Morty.

When Millie and Melody finish playing on the swings, they look up and see that they are alone.

"Hey, where did everyone go?"
Melody asks.

The girls find their friends on the soccer field.
"Why did you run off?" Millie asks.
"Because you and Melody were cutting in line and not taking turns," April explains. "If that's how you want to play…you can just play with each other!"

Millie and Melody look at each other. They want to play with everyone.

"We're sorry!" says Millie.

"We'll take turns from now on," Melody promises.

"That goes for us, too!"
Melody says to Millie.
"We can start by taking
turns with our things."
She hands her sister
the yellow backpack.

"And you can go first!"

Millie smiles and hands
her sister the teddy bear.

"And you can go first too!"

Both girls agree:
It's way more fun
to play fair!